W9-AFY-276

ROBERT SABUDA

ATHENEUM BOOKS for YOUNG READERS

To Jon Lanman

for his guidance, patience, and faith

—R. S.

Atheneum Books for Young Readers An imprint of Simon & Schuster Children's Publishing Division 1230 Avenue of the Americas New York, New York 10020 Book design by Michael Nelson. The text of this book is set in Vendome. The illustrations are rendered in batik. Printed in Hong Kong.
10 9 8 7 6 5 4 3 2
Library of Congress Cataloging-in-Publication Data: Sabuda, Robert. The blizzard's robe / written and illustrated by Robert Sabuda.—1st ed. p. cm. Summary: A young girl living in a village in the cold, dark Arctic north makes a robe for the feared Blizzard, and as a reward he creates the Northern Lights. ISBN 0-689-31988-6 [1. Arctic regions—Fiction.] I. Title. PZ7.S1178Bl 1999 [E]—dc21 98-36630

The artwork was created using a centuries-old technique called *batik*. Wax is applied to paper or silk and acts as a resist, preventing colored dye from penetrating the fiber. Subsequent layers of wax and dye are repeatedly applied to build up a multicolored picture.

FAR TO THE NORTH BY THE GREAT ARCTIC SEA, there once lived a clan of people. During the coldest part of winter, these people lived in almost total darkness because the angle of the sun, far to the south, just missed greeting their village each day. If the sun did rise above the horizon, it was for only a brief time, like a great whale rising to the surface of the sea for a quick breath.

The people feared this time of darkness, most of all because with it came terrible Blizzard, which could destroy anything with its icy winds and snow. Early on, the people came to be known as "the People Who Fear the Winter Night." And among these people there lived a young girl named Teune.

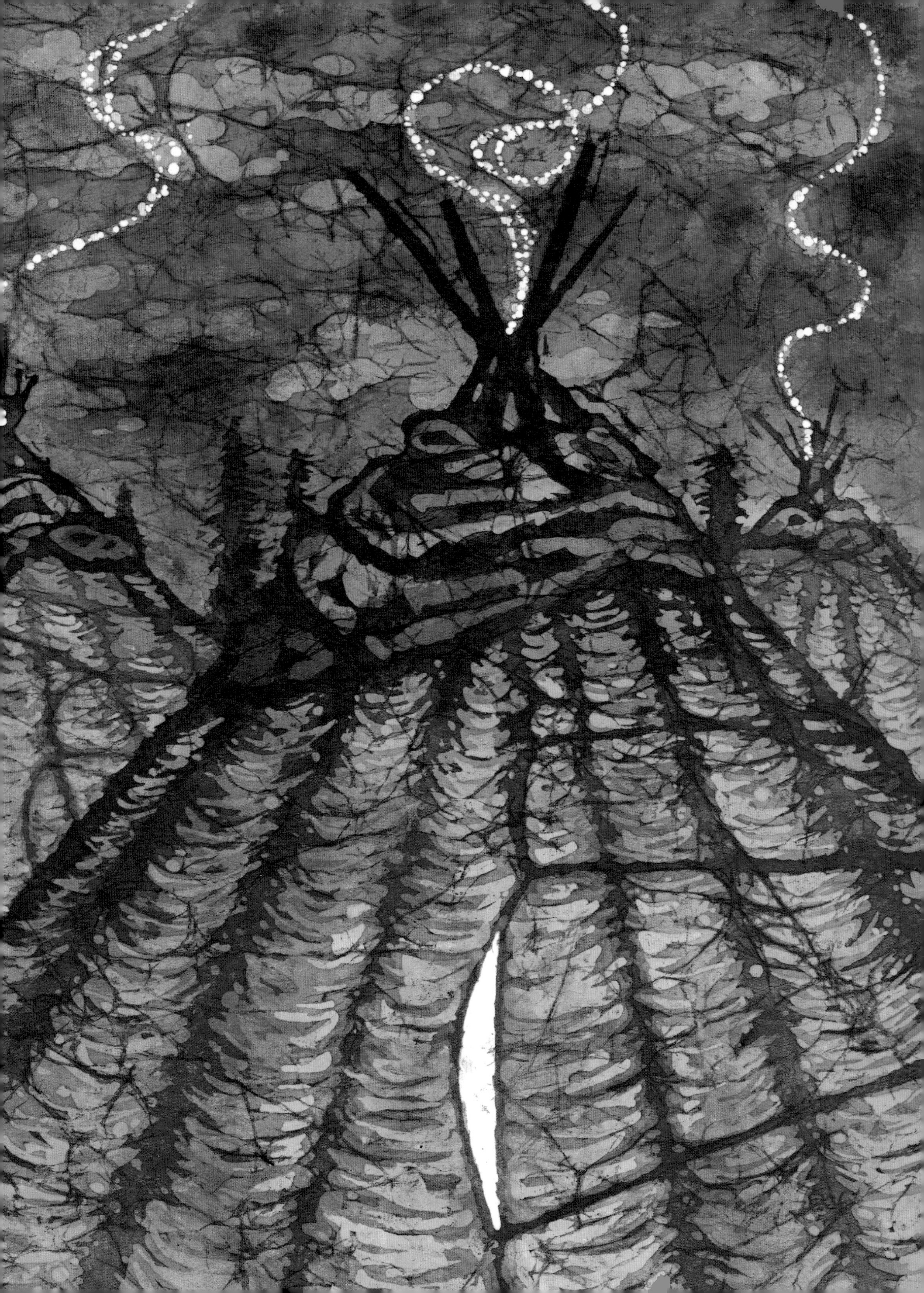

During the spring and summer and fall, while the other children were fishing or playing, Teune would sit by the hearth in her small *yaranga,* making robes to keep her people warm once winter arrived. Some were made of doeskin, white as snow. Others were as dark as the fearful Winter Night, embellished with brilliant designs.

"She is the finest robemaker I have ever seen," said the leader of the People Who Fear the Winter Night. And everyone in the village agreed.

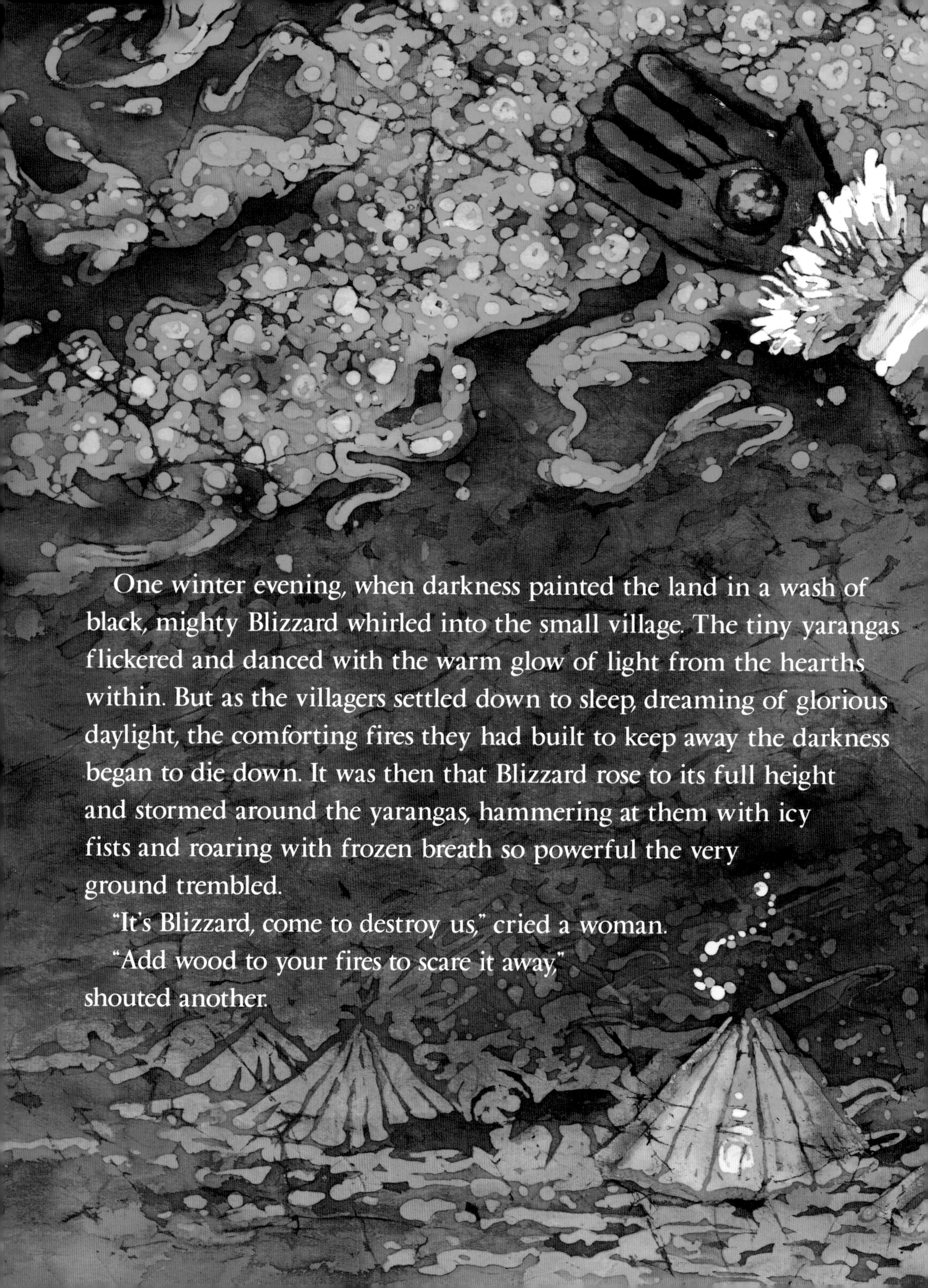

One winter evening, when darkness painted the land in a wash of black, mighty Blizzard whirled into the small village. The tiny yarangas flickered and danced with the warm glow of light from the hearths within. But as the villagers settled down to sleep, dreaming of glorious daylight, the comforting fires they had built to keep away the darkness began to die down. It was then that Blizzard rose to its full height and stormed around the yarangas, hammering at them with icy fists and roaring with frozen breath so powerful the very ground trembled.

"It's Blizzard, come to destroy us," cried a woman.

"Add wood to your fires to scare it away," shouted another.

Blizzard shrieked across the village, swirling from one yaranga to the next. The People Who Fear the Winter Night cried out as Blizzard's furious wind extinguished, one by one, the fires in their hearths. Soon they were enveloped by the vast, black Winter Night.

In Teune's yaranga there was no more wood to add to her fire. In her desperation to keep out Blizzard, she snatched up all her deerskins and stacked them atop the dying embers. Suddenly a great burst of sparks raced through the smoke hole at the top of her yaranga and out into the night.

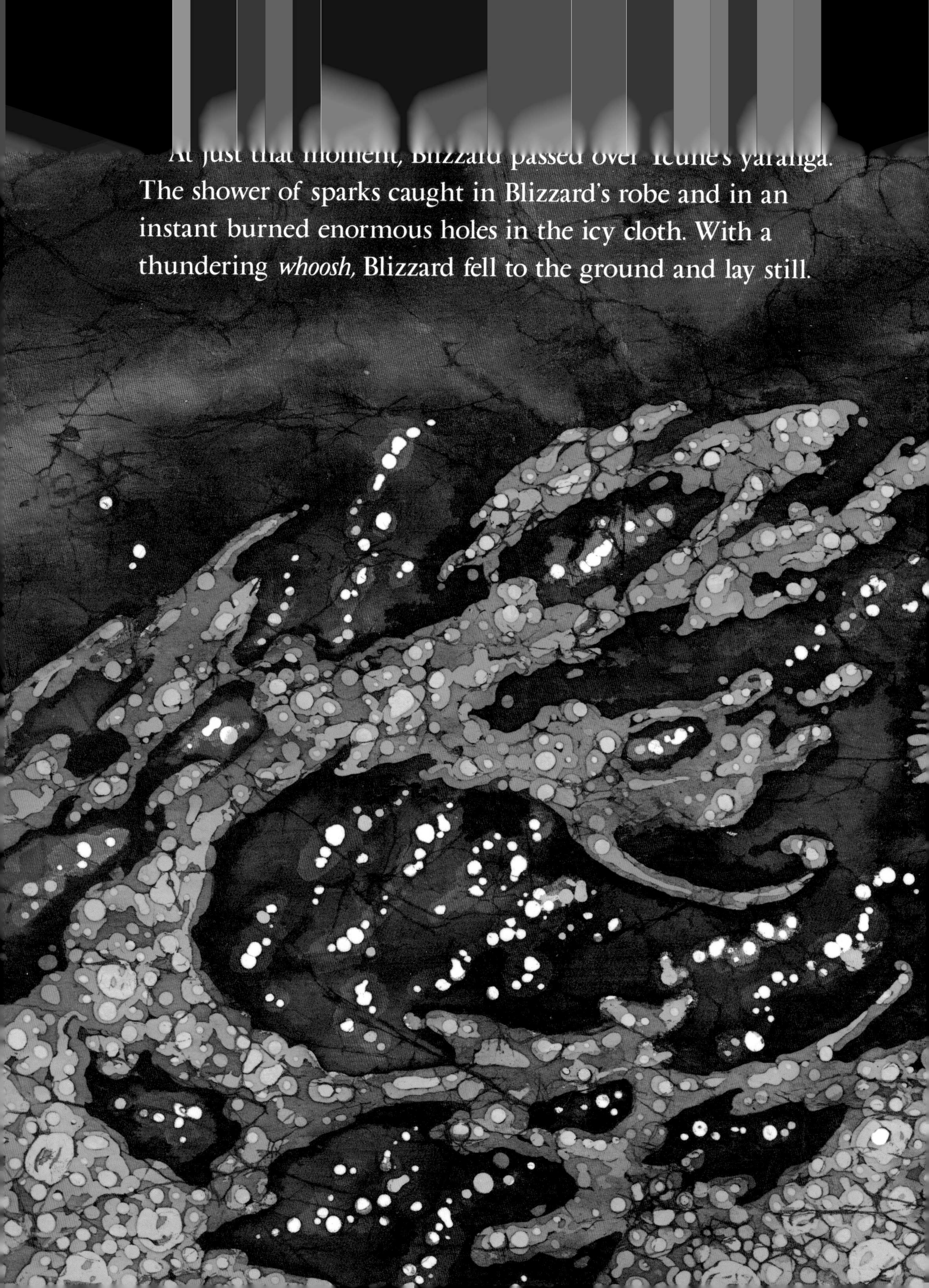

At just that moment, Blizzard passed over Tcune's yaranga. The shower of sparks caught in Blizzard's robe and in an instant burned enormous holes in the icy cloth. With a thundering *whoosh,* Blizzard fell to the ground and lay still.

The next morning, as the horizon was briefly pierced with light from the elusive sun, the villagers slowly gathered around the fallen Blizzard.

"Its robe has been destroyed," said one man. "Now it can no longer bring freezing misery into our village."

"We now have one less thing to fear from the Winter Night," said their leader, as the crowd turned and walked away.

Except for Teune. The girl approached the giant Blizzard and felt deep sadness in her heart. She still feared Blizzard,

almost as much as the Winter Night. But look at Blizzard's magnificent robe!

Teune had seen it only once before, when she was nearly trapped outside during one of Blizzard's terrible visits. Its frigid expanse had flowed endlessly, like the waves of the Arctic Sea. Now, lying on the ground, the robe was nothing more than a blackened mass of ice. Teune's eyes filled with tears. The villagers were happy Blizzard was no more, and she knew she should be as well. In fact, she was probably a hero to them. But she did not feel like one.

That night, Teune had a dream. In the dream, Blizzard flew into her tiny yaranga, but the flames in her hearth did not go out and the air stayed warm.

"Daughter of the People Who Fear the Winter Night," said Blizzard, "imagine that you wander on the vast arctic plain. Imagine that your voice roars like cracking ice, sending fear into the hearts of others. Imagine that your face is cold and made of ice. But imagine, too, that you are alone. Imagine that you are me."

Blizzard slowly drifted up toward the yaranga's smoke hole.

"I am what I must be. Please help me, Teune," it whispered, "and I will honor your people with the greatest gift."

When Teune awoke, she stepped outside and saw at her feet rolls of cloth and needles, but the cloth seemed made of ice. Remembering her dream, she picked them up and went back inside. As soon as she set the cloth down by the hearth, it began to melt. So she hurried back outside again. In the dim light, Teune could work only a few minutes at a time before her small hands became stiff with cold. But slowly she began to make a robe. She put designs of great frozen trees on the sleeves and pictures of the People Who Fear the Winter Night near the collar. On the hem of the skirt she placed stars, scattered across the Winter Night.

Going about their daily business, villagers passed by Teune's yaranga.

"Little robemaker," said an old woman, "what beautiful things do you make today? And why are you sitting out here when you should be inside, close to the hearth?"

A young mother approached with her child. "What a lovely robe. Perhaps if you have some deerskin left, you can make another like it for my boy."

The child touched the robe and quickly pulled away his hand. "It's ice!" he cried.

Teune simply smiled and continued to sew.

Soon word spread throughout the village that the little robemaker was creating something unusual. A robe with embroidery unlike any they had seen before, but that froze fingers at a touch.

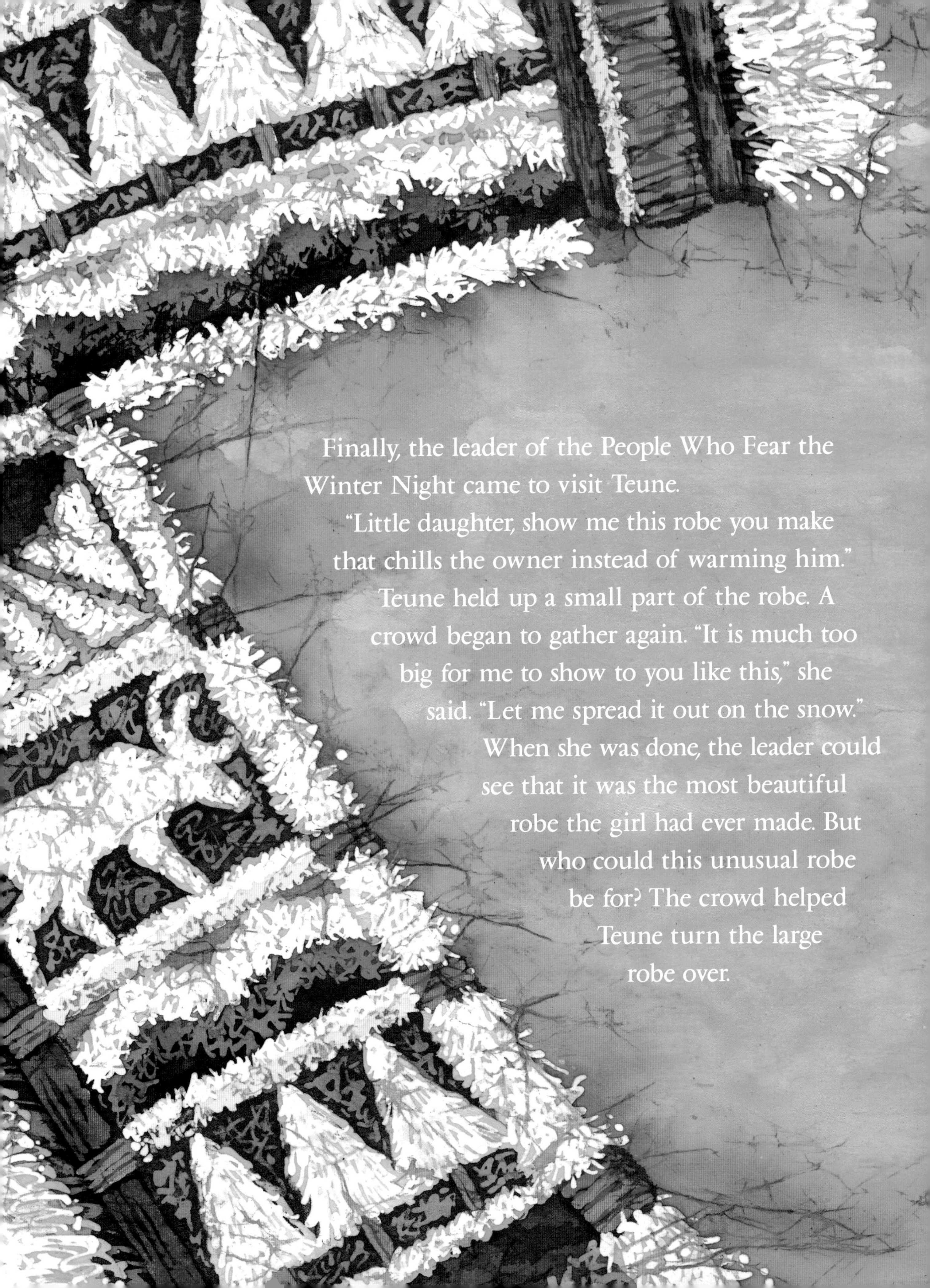

Finally, the leader of the People Who Fear the Winter Night came to visit Teune.

"Little daughter, show me this robe you make that chills the owner instead of warming him."

Teune held up a small part of the robe. A crowd began to gather again. "It is much too big for me to show to you like this," she said. "Let me spread it out on the snow."

When she was done, the leader could see that it was the most beautiful robe the girl had ever made. But who could this unusual robe be for? The crowd helped Teune turn the large robe over.

Covering the entire back was an enormous picture of Blizzard, shimmering like an ocean of diamonds.

"You have made this robe for Blizzard!" accused the leader, as the wind began to dance more briskly around him.

"Sparks from my hearth destroyed its first one. It was only right for me to replace it. And Blizzard promised a great gift for our people," cried Teune, straining to be heard above the suddenly rushing air.

"What kind of gift could Blizzard give us?" shouted the leader. He turned to the villagers. "Build a fire and destroy this robe at once."

But by now the wind had risen to a tremendous roar, and all at once it lifted the robe high above the village. As the robe fell to earth again, it gently floated down to where the motionless Blizzard was lying and covered him completely. Suddenly Blizzard rose, soared high into the sky, and streaked into the distance.

That night Teune lay awake. She gazed up through the yaranga's smoke hole, shivering at the sight of the Winter Night.

But something was different. Warm light seemed to slowly dance across the darkness. The girl hurried outside and saw others as well, rejoicing and pointing upward. Colored waves of light washed over the once-dreaded Winter Night, illuminating the entire village. Winter Night was dressed in a brilliant, colorful robe of its own that flowed from horizon to horizon! The villagers laughed and cried with happiness, for if this were indeed a gift from Blizzard, they could fear him less and accept the Winter Night.

And in the years that followed, every time the colored lights appeared, the villagers danced and sang praises for the little robemaker, whose kindness had brought the gift. A gift to those no longer called the People Who Fear the Winter Night, but the People of the Northern Lights.